Written and
Illustrated By
DAViD GOLDiN

HARRY N. ABRAMS, INC., PUBLISHERS

Today was the day,
the bicycle race
held once a year.
Maurice had to hurry!
He knew this time he would win the gold cup.

Feeling **lucky**,

he **rushed** to the park...

...and pulled into his place at **the starting line.**

"Hey Maurice," called out Stinky.
"Hope you're ready to lose on
that **old** clunk**e**r!"
"GO·GO·GO!"
cheered
the crowd.

"Get **ready**," called the announcer. "Get set. **GO!**" Maurice pedaled

"**GO·GO·GO!**" **roared** the crowd.
Maurice pedaled even

ast as he could.

faster.

Suddenly **trouble** crept across the road.
Maurice **SLAMMED** on his brakes,
swerving out of control.

He t^u**m**b^l**e**d and bo**u**n^c**e**d, barely hanging onto his wheels.

"Give up! You'll never win,"
Stinky snickered as he and the others *raced* on.

"Hold on!" hollered the crowd.

"GO·GO·GO!"

Back on course,
Maurice **ZOO**MED along.
He knew this was the year
he would win the gold cup.

"That's the **spirit**,"
cheered the crowd. "GO·GO·GO!"

"Out of my way!"
snarled Stinky.

"GO·GO·GO!"
yelled the crowd.

Go he did. Up, up and away.

"So long," waved Stinky.

Maurice **pedaled**. He **pushed**. He **pumped**. (And he held his breat

e **refuSed** to quit, because this year he knew **he would win** the gold cup.

Waterlogged and gasping for air,

Maurice raced on.

BA-*Bo*O**M** went the band (and *Maurice* on his bike).

Maurice was in last place.

Grunting and *groaning* he struggled **up** the **final hill**. His legs felt like **LEAD**.

He wondered **IF** this was the time he would win the gold cup. But he would not stop.

Coming over the rise,

wheels wobbling,

he began to *pick up* speed.

Down below was the finish line.

"GO·GO·GO!" the crowd roared.

Through the air Maurice sailed,

...*straight* across the finish **line.**

This time he **DID** win the gold cup.
Maurice was
the **champion!**

What a race! "Wait till next yea

"When on
a bicycle,
always wear
a helmet."

dedicated to: Weiner, Beanie, Pip, and...little Ella

special thanks to: Esther Pearl Watson, Mark Todd,
Howard Reeves, and of course, Amy.

Artist's Note
Late at night, when most people are asleep, the wheels in
my head start turning. My mind starts racing with ideas, so I
grab a pen and ink and watercolors and stay up to draw. I also
take anything I can find—bits of newspaper, bottle caps, old
labels, stamps—and glue it to the drawing to give more texture.
In the morning there is paper everywhere, covered with stories,
doodles, and creatures that I'd conjured up in the night.
—D.G.

You may visit David Goldin's website at: **www.Goldin.net**

Library of Congress Cataloging-in-Publication Data

Goldin, David.
    Go-Go-Go! / written and illustrated by David Goldin.
      p. cm.
    Summary: Maurice faces several obstacles as he works hard to win the annual bicycle race.
    ISBN 0-8109-4141-4
    [1. Bicycles and bicycling—Fiction. 2. Racing—Fiction.] I. Title.

PZ7.G56745 Go 2000
[E]—dc21   99-88544

Published in 2000 by Harry N. Abrams, Incorporated, New York

Printed and bound in Belgium

Design by Roger Gorman

Harry N. Abrams
100 Fifth Avenus
New York, N.Y. 10011
www.abramsbooks.com